The king was excited and asked the miller to bring his daughter to the castle. There he put her in a room with straw and a spindle and ordered her to spin the straw into gold by the next morning. But she did not know how to spin straw into gold.

STERLING CHILDREN'S BOOKS
New York

An Imprint of Sterling Publishing
387 Park Avenue South
New York, NY 10016

ISBN 978-1-4027-8340-1

Distributed in Canada by Sterling Publishing
c/o Canadian Manda Group, 165 Dufferin Street
Toronto, Ontario, Canada M6K 3H6
Distributed in the United Kingdom by GMC Distribution Services
Castle Place, 166 High Street, Lewes, East Sussex, England BN7 1XU
Distributed in Australia by Capricorn Link (Australia) Pty. Ltd.
P.O. Box 704, Windsor, NSW 2756, Australia

For information about custom editions, special sales, and premium and corporate
purchases, please contact Sterling Special Sales at 800-805-5489
or specialsales@sterlingpublishing.com.

Printed in China

Lot #:
2 4 6 8 10 9 7 5 3 1
01/14

www.sterlingpublishing.com/kids

SILVER PENNY STORIES

Rumpelstiltskin

Told by Deanna McFadden

Illustrated by Maurizio Quarello

Once upon a time there lived a poor miller who went to see the king. The miller wanted to impress the king, so he lied and said his beautiful daughter could spin straw into gold.

Tears fell down her cheeks. A gnome heard her crying and came into the room. When he asked her what was wrong, she told him about her impossible task.

The gnome said he could help, but he wanted a gift in return. So the miller's daughter gave him her pretty necklace. The gnome went to work, and soon the room was full of spun gold.

The next morning the king smiled at the sight of all the gold. He took the miller's daughter into an even larger room filled with straw. Again, he gave her until morning to spin it into gold.

The poor girl began crying, and the gnome appeared in the room. Again, he offered to spin the straw into gold and asked for a gift in return. The miller's daughter gave the gnome her bracelet, and he went right to work.

When the king opened the door the next morning, he couldn't believe his eyes. The room was full of spun gold. He took the miller's daughter to the biggest room he had. Straw was piled from floor to ceiling.

This time the king told the miller's daughter he would marry her if she could spin all the straw into gold. She sat down on the straw and cried for the third time.

The gnome appeared.

"What will you give me to spin this straw into gold?" he asked.

"I have nothing left to give," said the miller's daughter.

The gnome laughed. "Then I will take your first child after you become queen," he said.

The miller's daughter never believed she would become the queen, so she agreed. The gnome set to work and spun every last piece of straw into gold before morning.

When the king saw all the magnificent gold, he made her his queen.

A year later, she gave birth to a beautiful baby girl. The gnome appeared and said to her, "I'm here to take your child."

The queen begged him not to make her keep the promise. She told the gnome he could have all the riches in the kingdom.

"I will give you three days," he said. "If you can guess my name, you may keep your child."

When he came back the next day, the queen was prepared. She listed off every name that came to mind.

"Casper? Melchior? Balthazar?" she guessed.

The gnome smiled. "None of those is my name," he said as he left.

All night the queen asked the people of the kingdom to give her names. When the gnome arrived at the palace the next day, she asked, "Is your name Ribfiend or Muttonchops or Spindleshanks?"

Again, the gnome laughed.

"No!" he said. "None of those is my name."

That evening, the queen sent a
messenger out to search far and
wide for more names. When
he returned, he told her he had
traveled deep into the forest.

"I came upon a little hut," the messenger said, "where a gnome was dancing and singing around a glowing fire."

The messenger told the queen the song he had overheard:

"Oh, what luck to win this game!
Rumpelstiltskin is my name."

The queen was so happy! When the gnome appeared the next day she asked him, "Is your name Harry?"

He shook his head.

"Ethan?"

"No."

"Rumpelstiltskin?"

"How did you know?" the gnome shouted. "It's not fair!"

Then he ran out of the palace, never to return. The queen's little baby girl grew up to be a beautiful princess, and the name of Rumplestiltskin was never heard again.